What Makes God Smile?

LITTLE SIMON INSPIRATIONS

An imprint of Simon & Schuster Children's Publishing Division

1230 Avenue of the Americas, New York, New York 10020

Text copyright © 2005 by Karen Hill

Illustrations copyright © 2005 by Philomena O'Neill

All rights reserved, including the right of reproduction

in whole or in part in any form.

LITTLE SIMON INSPIRATIONS and associated colophon

are trademarks of Simon & Schuster, Inc.

Manufactured in the United States of America

First Edition

2 4 6 8 10 9 7 5 3 1

ISBN 1-4169-0514-6

Scripture taken from the *Holy Bible, New International Version*

copyright © 1973, 1978, 1984 by International Bible Society.

Used by permission of Zondervan Bible Publishers.

What Makes God Smile?

By Karen Hill
Illustrated by Philomena O'Neill

LITTLE SIMON INSPIRATIONS

New York   London   Toronto   Sydney

For our Ellie, our delight! —K. H.

For my sister, Geraldine, with love —P. O'N.

*"The fruit of the Spirit
is love, joy, peace, patience,
kindness, goodness, faithfulness,
gentleness and self-control."*

(Galatians 5: 22–23)

Ellie looked up from her breakfast of Fruity
Flakes.

"Mommy, what makes God smile?" the little
girl asked.

Mom placed a basket of muffins on the table.
"God smiles when *we* love like He loves," said
her mother.

Ellie jumped up. "Let's try to make God smile today!"

"Great idea!" Mom agreed.

"Will God smile if I'm a helper?" asked Ellie.

"Absolutely!" said Mom. "And I'll smile too!"

So Ellie put the napkins in the garbage and brought the breakfast plates to the sink.

When she was finished, Ellie went to play.
She took her map of America puzzle and
dumped the pieces on the floor.

Ellie loved putting puzzles together.

Her little sister, Emma, wanted to help.

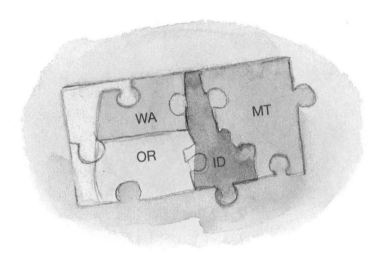

But Ellie wanted to do the puzzle all by
herself.

"Sharing makes God smile," reminded Mom.

Ellie thought and thought and thought some
more.

"Okay, you can help me with the puzzle,"
Ellie told Emma.

After awhile little Emma started acting silly.
She took the Texas piece and hid it under the
sofa. She stuck the California piece in her
pocket.

"Mom-meeee! Emma's bugging me!" Ellie
cried.

Mom said, "Be patient with your sister. She's younger than you are. That makes God smile."

Ellie thought and thought and thought some more.

She sighed, "All right. Emma, I'll show you where the pieces go."

Later Mom called, "Time to put your toys away. We're going to visit Grandma."

Emma didn't want to stop playing. "I don't want to go," she fussed.

Ellie thought and thought and thought some more.

She told her sister, "When we make Mommy smile, we make God smile too."

Emma helped Ellie pick up the puzzle pieces and put them away.

Before they left for Grandma's house, Mom said, "Let's think of ways to be extra nice to Grandma today—she's not feeling well."

Ellie thought and thought and thought some more.

"Can I draw a picture for her refrigerator?" asked Ellie.

"That's a wonderful idea," Mom said. "When we do nice things for others, we make God smile."

So Ellie drew a picture of Grandma in her garden.

Grandma smiled and said, "What a beautiful picture! I feel better already!"

That night Mommy tucked Ellie into bed.
She read Ellie's favorite book. They said their
prayers together, and as Mom tucked Ellie in,
she gave her a good-night kiss.

Ellie was quiet. She was thinking.

Then she asked, "Mommy . . . when you take care of me, are you making God smile?"

"*Hmmm*, yes, I guess I am," said Mom. "And when we make God smile, we can't help but smile too!"